NEW PUPPY ON THE BLOCK

By Jo Hurley
Illustrated by Jim Talbot

SCHOLASTIC INC.

New York   Toronto   London   Auckland   Sydney

Mexico City   New Delhi   Hong Kong   Buenos Aires

No part of this publication may be reproduced in whole or in part, stored in a retrieval system, or transmitted in any form or by any means, electronic, mechanical, photocopying, recording, or otherwise, without written permission of the publisher.
For information regarding permission, write to Scholastic Inc., Attention: Permissions Department, 557 Broadway, New York, NY 10012.

ISBN-13: 978-0-545-07903-7
ISBN-10: 0-545-07903-9

Littlest Pet Shop © 2009 Hasbro.

12 11 10 9 8 7 6 5 4 3 2 1   9 10 11 12 13 14/0

Designed by Angela Jun
Printed in the U.S.A.
First printing, March 2009

Contents

Chapter 1
Welcome to the Shop

Ding-a-ling! Ding-a-ling!

A doorbell jingled. All the animals inside the Littlest Pet Shop looked up to see who was at the door. The next big adventure was about to begin.

Yip! Yip! Yip!

A black-and-white Dalmatian trotted in through the pet shop doors for the first time. He poked his pink nose up in the air.

So this is my new home, he thought.

The Dalmatian looked around. There

Wa-woof!

was so much to see and do! There were cats and fish, gerbils and lizards, all playing, eating, and sleeping in different parts of the shop.

But where are all the puppies? he thought. The Dalmatian scampered over to the large pen at the front of the store.

Puppies! Hooray!

At the front of the store were two pups playing with a large purple ball. A bulldog pushed the ball with his nose. The Dalmatian let out a howl and pounced on the purple ball.

Rrrrrowf!

"Hey," howled the bulldog. "What are you doing? That's our ball!"

"I'm playing!" the Dalmatian barked cheerfully. His tail wagged back and forth as he jumped onto his back paws.

"Wheeee!"

"Excuse me," a Maltese with white fluffy fur yipped as she adjusted the pretty pink bows on her head.  "We were playing with that."

"Great! Let's play!" the Dalmatian yelped. He pushed the ball hard with his nose.

The two puppies stared.

"Isn't this fun?" the Dalmatian cried. He raced across the floor of the pen. Shredded newspaper flew into the air. It landed all over the Maltese.

"What a mess!" the Maltese said.

The Dalmatian barked as he grabbed the ball between his teeth. He shook it hard. The ball went flying up into the air, bounced on the counter, and soared right onto a high shelf of Bacon Bites.

"Oh, no!" the Maltese cried.

The puppies raced over to the shelf. The Dalmatian leaped into the air but he couldn't reach the top.

"Uh-oh," said the bulldog. "That was his favorite ball."

"It was an accident," said the Dalmatian. "I didn't mean to do it! Whose ball is it?"

"Aye! What's all the ruckus?" A Scottish terrier puppy dashed over. He had a shaggy beard, a funny accent, and a cute plaid cap. He was very upset. "Hey! That was my favorite ball," the Scottish terrier growled. "I loved it more than all the rawhide chews in the shop."

"I'm sorry," the Dalmatian said. "I was just trying to play."

The Scottish Terrier frowned.

"Don't worry about the ball," the bulldog said to the Scottish Terrier. "Let's play tag instead."

"I love tag! Let's go!" squealed the Maltese.

But the three puppies wandered away without the Dalmatian. He couldn't believe it!

"Whoa, wait for me!" the Dalmatian yelped. He zoomed after them like a race car. *Whooosh!* He slid across the shredded newspaper on the floor.

Kerthunk! Before he knew it, the Dalmatian had crashed face-first into another puppy.

"Yowch!" the puppy squealed from the corner. He was a German shepherd.

"Oh!" the Dalmatian said, surprised. "I didn't see you there."

"I was trying to sleep!" the German

shepherd barked with a scowl. "You should watch where you're going!"

The Dalmatian flopped down onto the floor of the pen and covered his eyes with his long ears.

"It's hard being a new puppy here," the Dalmatian said to himself. "Nobody wants to play with me."

The Dalmatian wondered if he would ever feel at home.

Chapter 2
Meet Tabby

The Dalmatian nosed around the pen, looking for other things to do. There were so many smells in here: other puppies and chew toys and the layer of wood chips underneath the newspaper. He even found a little loose kibble near a row of dog dishes and ate it.

It was fun to explore! The Dalmatian headed toward the back of the store. The lights in the shop were shining now. Outside, it was getting dark. Night was approaching, but the pup didn't want to go to sleep. Not yet.

Against one wall, the new pup saw a row of beds. Other animals were sleeping. He tiptoed over and saw an empty bed. There was a sign in front of it that said DALMATIAN.

Dalmatian

"Go ahead, take a look inside. That spot is just for you," a voice said.

The Dalmatian jumped. "Who's there?"

A tabby cat appeared out of the shadows. She smiled and batted her deep blue-green eyes.

"Hello," the tabby cat mewed. "Don't worry. I don't scratch."

The Dalmatian laughed and wagged his tail. "Hello! I'm the new puppy in the shop."

The tabby cat nodded. "I know. I've been watching you."

"I've never talked to a cat before," the Dalmatian admitted.

"Cats and dogs aren't all that different," the tabby cat explained. "Except that cats are smarter, better looking, and much nicer than most dogs, but—"

"Hey! Dogs are nice, too," the Dalmatian said boldly.

"Of course dogs are nice! I'm just pulling your tail!" The tabby cat purred with delight.

The Dalmatian frowned and hung his head down sadly. "But the puppies

here haven't been so nice to me," he said. "They didn't invite me to play ball or tag with them."

"Don't worry," said the tabby with a kind voice. "The other animals just need time to get to know you. Then they'll understand what a great friend you can be."

The Dalmatian smiled. "That makes me feel a little better."

"Great!" the tabby cat said, stretching out her legs. "Now let's take a tour of the Littlest Pet Shop. Everyone here calls me Tabby because I'm a tabby cat!"

"I like that!" panted the Dalmatian.

"We'll call you . . ." Tabby mewed, "Dally! You'll have a bunch of new friends in no time, Dally. Just you wait!"

Chapter 3
Looking Around

The sky was getting dark. Dally and Tabby could just barely see the store's front window.

"I love twilight time," whispered Tabby. "Sometimes the Littlest Pet Shop owner leaves out a special snack before she goes."

"Where does she go?" asked Dally.

"Home. Every night after seven o'clock, she closes the store and leaves for the day."

"Oh," Dally said. "Do you miss her?"

"Of course we do!" mewed Tabby. "But the Littlest Pet Shop is fun at night, too."

"I bet it is!" Dally said.

Dally and Tabby walked past food and toy displays. They talked about the things cats enjoy, like balls of yarn, cat toys, and tuna fish salad.

"I like Bacon Bites, chasing my tail, and playing tag!" Dally cried. Playfully, he poked Tabby with his oversized, spotted paw. "You're it!" Dally ran around in a circle, chasing his tail.

"*Ssshhh.* Not so loud," Tabby purred, arching her back. "We can't play here."

"Why not?" Dally asked.

"A lot of the pets are settling down to sleep," said Tabby.

"But I'm not tired at all!" Dally said, jumping from one paw to the other.

Tabby mewed. "We can play tag later, Dally."

Dally panted. He was still a little overexcited. "Okay. I guess I can wait."

Tabby walked along a wall. "Watch

your step," she said to Dally. She led the way to an enormous pen.

Hanging on the wall was a huge sign that read: CAT WORLD. Inside, Dally saw snoozing cats, cat toys, and scratching posts.

"Watch your step," said Tabby as she led Dally inside. "You don't want to step on any tails."

Inside the cage, Dally heard humming sounds. "It sounds like cat music!"

Tabby laughed. "Yes, if you call a bunch of cats snoring *music*," she cried, "then this is a regular cat orchestra."

"Hello, cats!" Dally called out.

Tabby quickly leaped onto Dally and knocked him over. "*Shhhhhh!*" she said. "You have to be very, very quiet here. Never disturb a sleeping cat."

Carefully, Tabby pawed her way over to a small box. She poked inside and came out with something in her mouth. It was a pink pocketbook.

"What's in there?" Dally asked.

"My favorite things," Tabby replied. With the flick of a paw, Tabby opened her purse.

"Let me see!" barked Dally. He dove into Tabby's purse.

"Be careful!" Tabby mewed.

But it was too late! When he tried to pull out his snout, it got stuck. He yanked his head up. *How could he free himself from the bag?* Dally twirled and tossed his body from side to side. He shook as hard as he could.

At last, the bag flew off. But everything inside went flying, too!

There were fish crackers and Bacon Bites and little rubber toys. There were balls of yarn and strings of bells. Everything went flying up and landed all over the floor.

Clang! Thunk! Rattle!

All the cats woke up with the ruckus. They all started stretching and mewing at the same time. *Meow! Meow! Meowwwww!* The cranky cats stretched up and stormed over, surrounding Dally. He was so startled, he didn't know which way to run. He ran around and around in a circle, spinning like a dog tornado. As he bounced back and forth, he got all tangled up in a big ball of yarn.

What a mess! The more Dally tried to free himself from the string, the more he got tied in knots. Off in the corner, he saw the Maltese giggling at

him. How embarrassing! Dally felt so silly with red yarn wrapped around his paws and head. He dashed away to the other corner.

"I'm sorry," he said to Tabby,

hanging down his head.

"It's all right," said Tabby. "You just have to be a little more careful."

Lucky for him, Tabby was an expert at untangling string. Dally didn't mention seeing the Maltese. He didn't want to tell Tabby that he felt nervous around the other puppies.

After she got Dally unknotted, Tabby clapped her paws together. "Let's go! We'll pick up the rest of this mess later. It's time to visit Hamster Land! I think you'll like the hamsters. They like to play as much as you," Tabby said.

Dally's eyes lit up. "*Rooowf!*" he barked. "I can't wait."

Chapter 4
Circus Tricks

Dally saw the sign: HAMSTER LAND. Inside were wood shavings, water bottles, hamster tunnels, and a collection of the cutest hamsters ever. Tiny, furry hamsters were running on little plastic wheels.

"The hamsters are all wide awake!" Dally exclaimed.

"They're nocturnal," said Tabby. "That means they wake up and play at night. They have a nightly show we call our Littlest Pet Shop Circus."

"Wow," said the Dalmatian. "Is there a circus tonight?"

"You bet there is! Every night!" squealed a hamster jogging on one of the hamster wheels. She had a little rainbow-colored sweatband on her head.

"That's Hammy," said Tabby. "And she is a real ham. She likes to be the center of attention.

"Hamsters in the Littlest Pet Shop are great performers. I always come to watch," explained Tabby.

Dally was thrilled. Finally he was meeting pets who liked to play.

"Hello!" Dally cried to the hamsters.

Two more hamsters came down to talk to Dally. One hamster was golden yellow. The other was brown. They poked their hamster heads out of the cage.

"I'm Goldie. Pleased to meet you," said the yellow hamster. Dally noticed how busy Goldie was. She didn't stop wiggling, nibbling on her paw, or

combing her fur.

"What's your name?" Dally asked the brown hamster.

"I'm Mr. Brown," he said.

Mr. Brown and Goldie were soon joined by Hammy. They asked Tabby to be the emcee for tonight's circus show. Tabby happily agreed.

The hamster trio scampered away to set up their trapeze and their tightrope. Other hamsters put out chairs for the guests. From outside the cage, Tabby prepared her announcement.

"Presenting . . ." Tabby purred. "Triple Trouble!"

Dally leaned back, grinning from

spotted ear to spotted ear. What a show! Hammy took center stage first. She did a cartwheel. Then she hopped onto the hamster wheel and did another cartwheel while it was moving.

"Wow!" cried Dally. "That's incredible!"

Goldie did a somersault onto her hamster wheel. Mr. Brown stood on his head.

"Watch closely!" cried Tabby.

"What's going to happen next?" asked Dally.

Goldie climbed onto Mr. Brown's shoulders. Then Hammy climbed on top of Mr. Brown and Goldie! They were three hamsters high!

"Oooooooh!" cooed the hamster audience.

"Oooooooh!" said Dally. He leaped to his feet and cheered, "Go! Go! Go!"

The three hamsters teetered and tottered, but they stayed up.

"Ta-da!" they shouted.

"Now it's time for our amazing maze trick," Mr. Brown said. He pointed to the plastic hamster tunnels.

"Oh, can I join you?" Dally asked eagerly. He zoomed toward the hamster tunnels.

"Welcome to the circus!" everyone cried. "Any friend of Tabby's is a friend of ours."

Dally could see the other three hamsters running into the tunnels around him. Here was his chance to play tag—at last! But when he tried to wiggle inside the plastic tunnel, he could only fit his snout! Dally stepped back from the tunnel and saw something even better! A ball! He had never seen a ball like this before. He ran over excitedly to play with it.

"No, Dally!" cried Tabby. But it was too late! Dally had given the ball a swift kick. He didn't realize there was a hamster inside it!

"Stop that ball!" Tabby called as the ball rolled out of control. A crowd of hamsters scampered in front of the moving ball and blocked it from rolling farther. They opened a latch and out

crawled a dizzy hamster.
The hamster stumbled to the left and then to the right. Then he fell down.

Oh, no! Dally thought. He couldn't believe he had made such a mistake! Without a word, he ran straight for the exit. He felt too bad to even wait for Tabby.

"We saw that. We were watching you!" Dally turned around to see who was talking. He couldn't believe his eyes. It was the bulldog! The bulldog and the Maltese had seen him kick the hamster ball. Dally didn't know what to say, so he just dashed away with his head hung low. This was even worse than what had happened in Cat World.

"Hey," Tabby called after Dally. "Wait for me!"

Dally stopped to wait for Tabby.

"Don't worry. That hamster was a little stunned, but he's just fine," Tabby said gently.

"Is there any place I can go where I won't cause trouble?" Dally asked sadly.

Chapter 5
Something Fishy

"Here are some new friends you will like," Tabby said as they walked on together. "You can play with them, but you can't make a mess," she continued with a grin.

Dally smiled. "Thanks, Tabby. You're a good friend."

"Everyone here is a good friend!" Tabby said. "We all started out as new pets in the shop. We were all embarrassed and nervous at first."

"You were?" Dally asked. "I can't

believe that."

"When I first arrived at the shop, I knocked down five hamsters with my tail," Tabby confessed. "They were afraid of me for weeks!"

Dally followed Tabby down into the main part of the Littlest Pet Shop. The aisles were dark but they came upon an enormous fish tank, all lit up. The water was filled with tropical fish in every color.

"Let's sit here awhile," Tabby said.

Tabby and Dally lay down on their backs and looked up at the tank. The whole tank looked blue and shimmered.

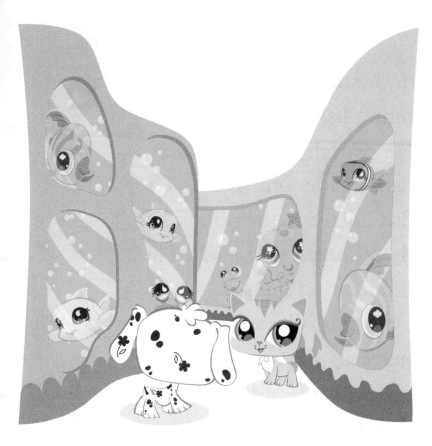

Tabby arched her back. "Cats don't like water. But I love coming here. It's like being under the sea without the wet part."

"Wow," said Dally. He rolled over

and stood up. "How many fish are in there?" He watched the orange fish inside one tank. The fish darted to the right. Then they darted to the left. They dipped and flipped.

"They all swim together!" Dally yelped.

"A group of fish is called a school," Tabby said.

Dally tried to copy them. "I always wanted to go to school." He giggled. He jumped up. He chased his tail. He leaped high into the air.

"Dally!" cried Tabby. "The fish like you. They're watching you!"

Dally laughed. He liked the fish, too. He waved to all the fish with his big puppy paw. He was amazed at how different they all were. There were fish with colored stripes. There were fat, small fish with silver scales. There was one enormous brown fish that hid under a rock. There was a whole group of black fish with white spots on their tails. There were even fish with spots on their fins that looked like eyes!

The tanks were decorated with plants and painted treasure chests that blew open with bubbles. Then Dally saw something he had never seen before.

"Who is that?" Dally asked Tabby. Dally stared at a strange creature inside one of the largest tanks. It looked like a fish on top. But it had a curly tail underneath.

"That's a sea horse," said Tabby.

"What's its name?" asked Dally.

Tabby shrugged. "I'm not sure. He's new, too."

"He's new here?" Dally exclaimed. "Like me?"

Tabby nodded. "He came to the Littlest Pet Shop last week. I only met him once."

The sea horse seemed to float in the water. Dally wanted to say hello. He tried to move like the fish in the other tanks. He raced around in a circle. He ran far away from the tanks. Then he raced forward at full speed.

Dally had forgotten all about the glass. He sat there stunned. "Ouch. My nose hurts a little," said Dally. "How did that happen?"

"You were excited," said Tabby. "You didn't see the glass!"

Inside the tank, the sea horse grinned.

"Fish you were in here!" the sea horse gurgled.

All the fish inside the tank laughed, but Dally thought they were laughing at him, not at the sea horse's joke.

He rubbed his face a little with one paw. His nose stung from when he smashed into the tank. But he felt even worse when he saw the grinning faces on the school of fish. He felt just like he did when he was inside the puppy pen. The only thing Dally was good at was making pets laugh at him!

Tabby took Dally by his paw. "Don't worry," she said, trying to make him

feel better. "Do you like music? I know another place where we can go."

Dally barked. "Let's go quickly before the fish start laughing at me again!"

Chapter 6
Bird Songs

As the pair scooted down another aisle, Dally saw bird playgrounds and giant bird feeders. A flock of birds dove in and pecked at the seed in the bird feeders. One bird began to whistle.

Tweetle tweet. Tweetle tweet.

"Hello!" Dally barked at the bird.

"Hi there!" called the bird. It was a beautiful bird with pink and yellow downy feathers.

Dally grinned. "Who are you?" he asked.

"Everyone at the shop calls me Pink!" she cried. "And who are you?"

"I'm Dally the Dalmatian," he said.

All the birds sang Dally's name at the exact same time.

Pink perched on a bird stand and announced to the group, "You're just in time, Dally. The singing contest is about to begin!"

A few birds flew away to get stage decorations. There was a plastic palm tree, a streamer made from purple crepe paper, and bags of confetti to throw into the air.

Tabby agreed to make the introductions, just as she had done at the hamster cages. "And now," crooned Tabby, "presenting . . . the Littlest Pet Shop Cabaret!"

"Wow," said Dally. "This is special!"

"Yes it is! We're all special," Tabby said. "Including you. You'll see!"

Pink began the show. She flapped her fluffy wings and belted out, "Crow, crow, crow your boat." Everyone cheered.

Next a group of three birds started to sing "Rockin' Robin." Dally clapped his paws to the beat. The birds were fantastic. Dally loved to move and dance. As the birds tweetily tweeted, he chased his tail in one direction, then the other. He stretched his back like the cats. He did somersaults like the hamsters.

In time to the music, he darted from side to side like the fish.

Suddenly he noticed a circle had formed around him. The birds were all pointing at him and laughing. Dally froze. *Oh, no!* he thought. *The birds are making fun of me just like all of the puppies and fish.*

Tabby dashed over. "That was GREAT, Dally!" she mewed. "The birds are all cheering for you. And they're not the only ones!" Tabby pointed down the aisle. The puppies were there, too.

Chapter 7
Puppy Power

The puppies headed toward him. Dally didn't know what to do.

"Just tell them how you feel," said Tabby. "Remember, they were new pups in the shop once, just like you."

The bulldog, Maltese, Scottish terrier, and German shepherd came over. Before they had a chance to speak, Dally blurted out, "I'm sorry for losing your ball and for crashing into you!"

The puppies looked at one another. Then they laughed.

"Oh, no! You're *still* laughing at me," Dally cried. He dropped to the floor and put his floppy ears over his eyes.

"We're not laughing *at* you!" explained the bulldog. "We're laughing because we came over here to apologize to *you*."

Dally looked confused. "You did?"

"We wanted to tell you this a long time ago," the Maltese went on. "But every time we tried to come over to you, you ran away."

"I did?" asked Dally.

"We saw how friendly you were playing with the cats, and the hamsters, and the fish, too," said the

Scottish terrier.

"We should have invited you to play with us," said the bulldog. "It wasn't nice to leave you behind."

"I shouldn't have gotten so upset about the purple bouncy ball," said the Scottish terrier. "I got another one. It's even better because it has stripes!"

"I'm not sorry for growling at you," said the German shepherd.

Dally's eyes got wide.

"Well, you did crash into me," joked

the German shepherd. "And I growl at all my friends!"

Dally started to smile.

"It's about time you got to know all your new friends," barked the bulldog. "I'm Bull." Then he pointed to the Scottish Terrier and the German shepherd. "That's Scotty and there's Shep."

"And I'm Malt!" cried the Maltese.

Dally twirled around and did another puppy dance.

"I knew you'd feel better!" mewed Tabby. "When someone feels scared or embarrassed—"

"Like me?" Dally interrupted.

"Yes. Like you," Tabby continued. "The Littlest Pet Shop is a great place to be. And it's not just for pets. This place can make *people* feel better, too."

"People?" asked Dally.

"Of course! We make visitors feel special, too. Because they are!"

Dally howled happily. "I can't believe I have so many new friends. I only wish the sea horse could be here, too—and all the fish."

"They can!" barked Bull.

The puppies gathered everyone together. "Everyone line up!" Bull cried. "Let's march on over to the fish tanks so the underwater crew can play, too!"

Everyone followed Bull to the fish

tanks. The puppies tossed and dribbled the ball as they marched. Malt tossed the ball high into the air. Dally caught it and balanced it on his nose like a seal.

"Nice trick!" said Bull. "Can you show me how to do that?"

"You bet!" said Dally. "And I've got a lot more tricks where that one came from. Just you wait and see!"

Tabby purred and all at once a group of cats appeared, rolling a ball of string in front of them. Other pets joined in from around the shop, too.

They reached the fish tanks. Everyone at the Littlest Pet Shop was together at last. But they still hadn't found their biggest surprise.

"Look! Over there!" Tabby purred. "The pet shop owner put out snacks for all of us!"

Near the fish tanks was a table loaded with special snacks: dog chews, bird seed, cat cookies, and more.

"Wow!" Dally yelped. "This is the best place in the whole world. Well . . . except for one little thing. . . ."

"What could that be?" Tabby asked, arching her back.

"Nobody has played tag yet! NOW can we play?" Dally cried.

Tabby laughed. "Oh, Dally . . ."

She stuck out her paw and tapped
him on the nose. "YOU'RE IT!"

Pet Profiles

List and describe Littlest Pet Shop pets from your collection—or put in facts about the pets from the story.

Littlest Pet	Special Talent(s)
A Dalmatian	Frisky, friendly, fun

Littlest Pet   ## Special Talent(s)

_____   _____

_____   _____

_____   _____

_____   _____

_____   _____

_____   _____

_____   _____

_____   _____

_____   _____

_____   _____

Making New Friends

Being new can be scary. Here are some tips and tricks for making new friends feel welcome.

· Don't judge a pet by its spots! Always get to know what a new friend is like on the inside.

· To speak or not to speak? Sometimes someone new can act a little bit shy. Give that friend a chance to open up! Others may be a little too excited at first. Give those new pals the chance to relax.

· Play around! Playing is a great way to get to know someone new. Ask questions. Be interested. Offer to share something—a game, a snack, or even a giggle.

· **Teach a new friend new tricks. Take turns showing a new friend your special talents. Then see what new things you can learn.**

The Fun Never Ends

What other adventures might Dally, Tabby, Bull, Scotty, Shep, and Malt have together? Write your own story here!

_____

_____

_____

_____

_____

_____

_____

_____

_____

_____

_____